THE BALL-HEADED MONSTERS

CREATED AND ILLUSTRATED BY DEREK GRAHAM

author**HOUSE**

AuthorHouse™
1663 Liberty Drive
Bloomington, IN 47403
www.authorhouse.com
Phone: 833-262-8899

Published by AuthorHouse 10/17/2024

ISBN: 979-8-8230-3284-1 (sc)
ISBN: 979-8-8230-3283-4 (e)

Library of Congress Control Number: 2024918341

Print information available on the last page.

This book is printed on acid-free paper.

SPIKEY BALL

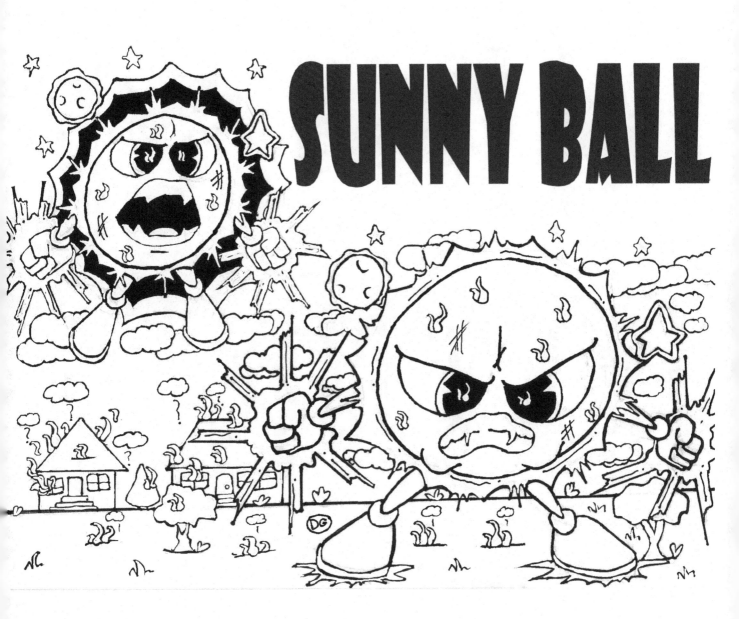

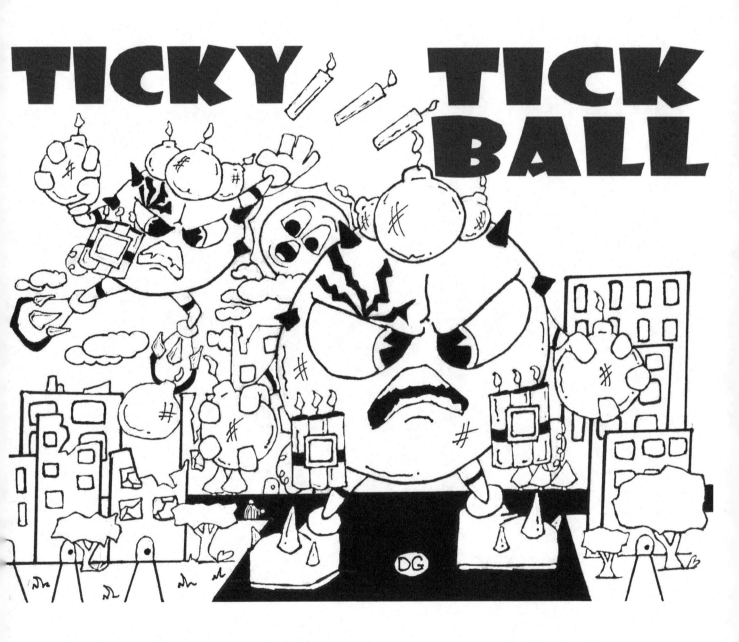

TWISTER BALL

WITCHY BALL

SEE-SEE BALL

SNAKEY BALL

SPIDEY BALL

MOTHY BALL

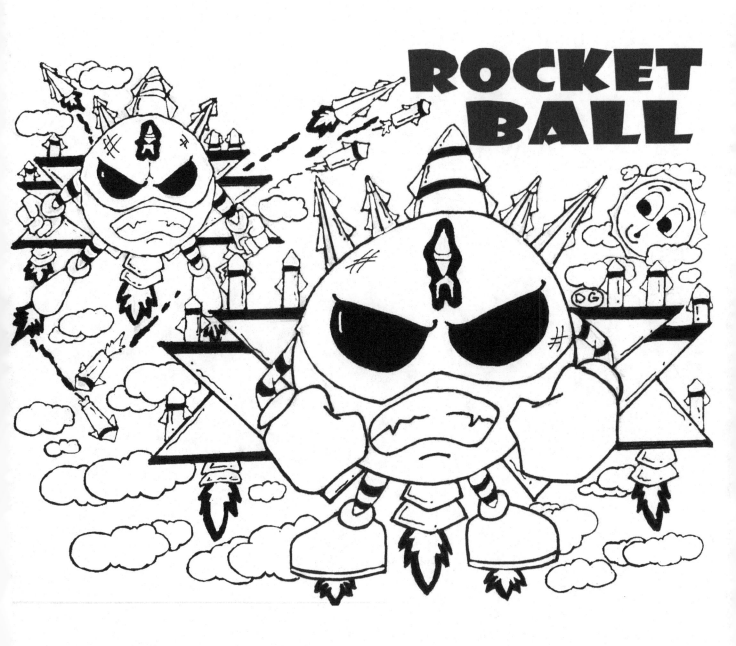

ICY BALL

BULLY BALL

CAPPY BALL

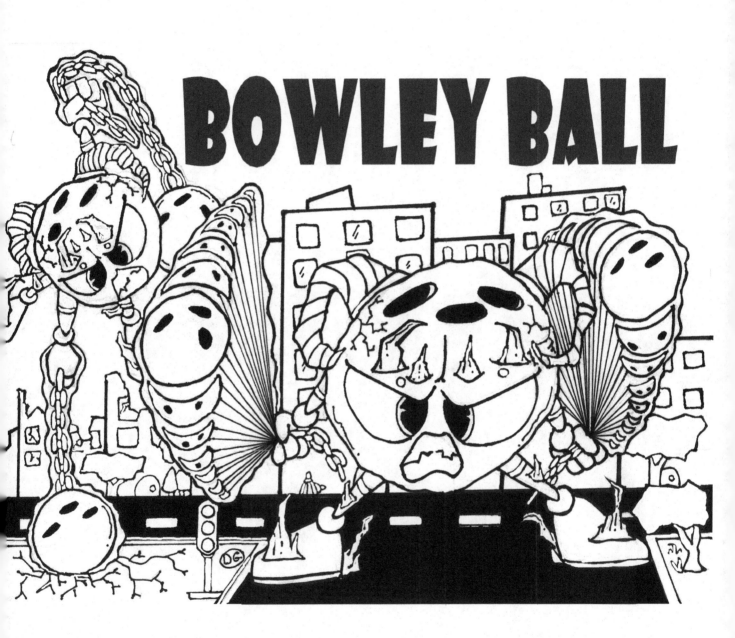

BALL BOTZ

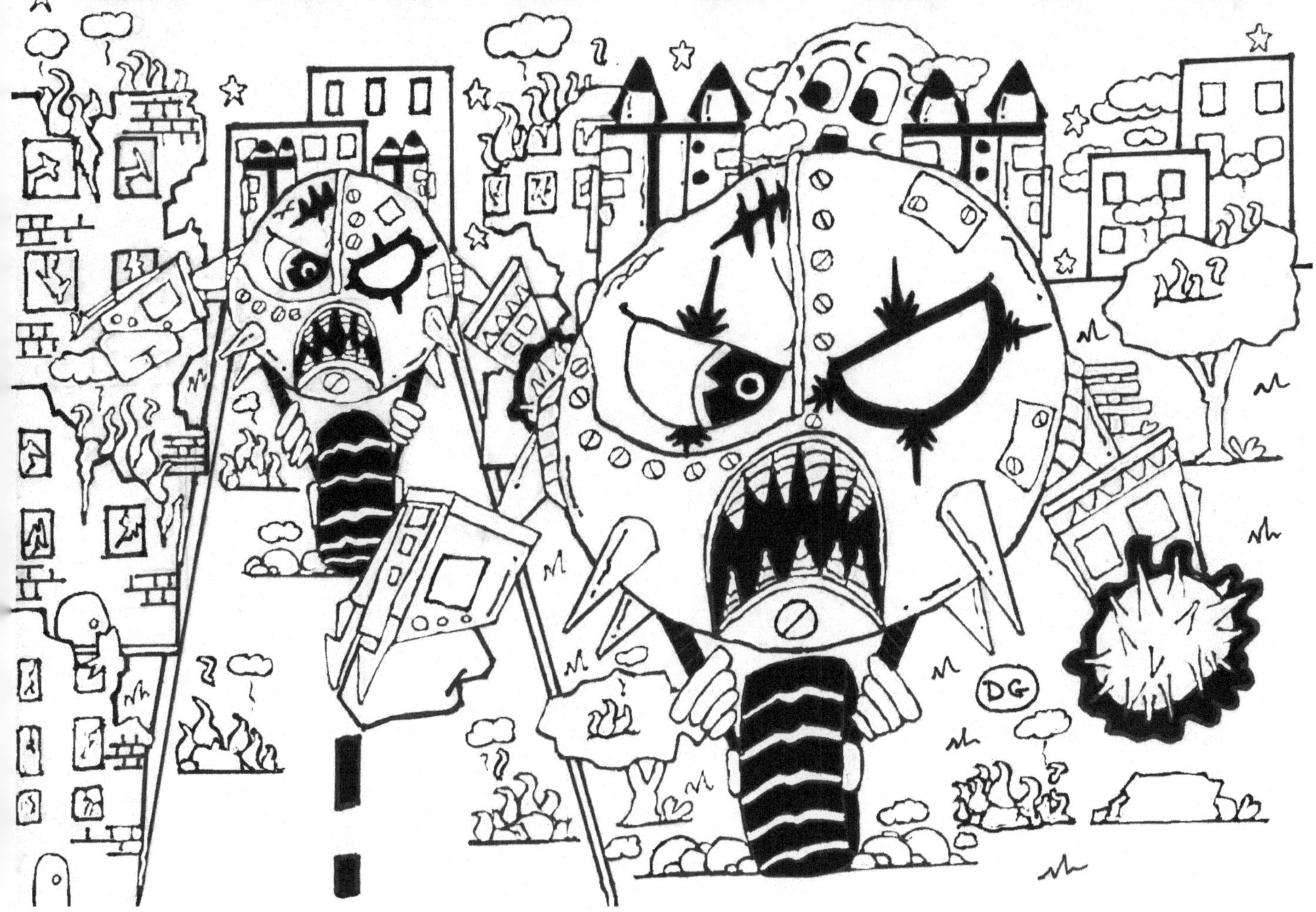

MUMMY BALL

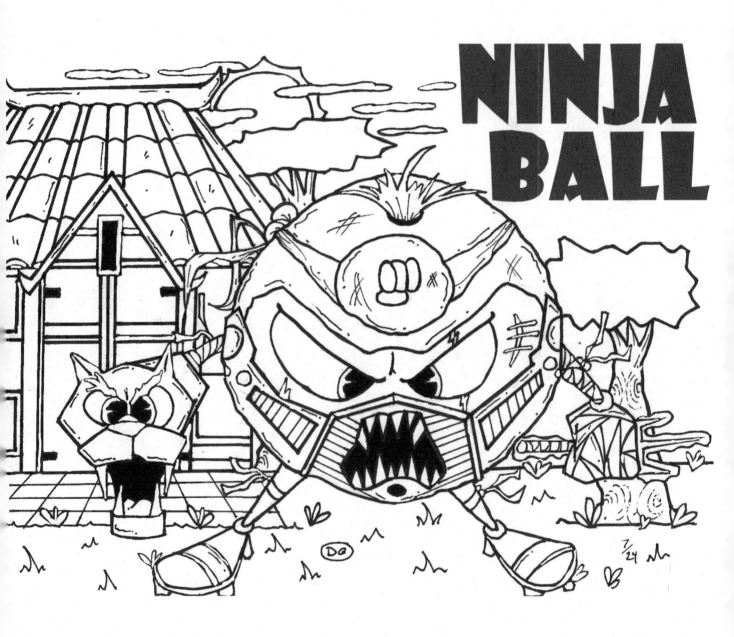

63

Printed in the United States
by Baker & Taylor Publisher Services